STERLING CHILDREN'S BOOKS
New York

An Imprint of Sterling Publishing Co., Inc.
1166 Avenue of the Americas
New York, NY 10036

Text and illustrations © 2018 Lucy Freegard

First Sterling edition published in 2019.
First published in the United Kingdom in 2018 by Pavilion Children's Books,
43 Great Ormond Street, London WC1N 3HZ.

ISBN 978-1-4549-3420-2

Distributed in Canada by Sterling Publishing Co., Inc.
c/o Canadian Manda Group, 664 Annette Street
Toronto, Ontario M6S 2C8, Canada

For information about custom editions, special sales, and premium and corporate purchases, please contact Sterling Special Sales at 800-805-5489 or specialsales@sterlingpublishing.com.

Manufactured in China
Lot #:
2 4 6 8 10 9 7 5 3 1
12/18

sterlingpublishing.com

Just Like Mommy

Lucy Freegard

STERLING CHILDREN'S BOOKS
New York

My friends say that when they grow up,
they want to be...

a doctor,

an astronaut,

and a firefighter.

But when I grow up, I want to be...

...just like Mommy!

I will know so many
things about the earth,

the sea, and...

...the stars in the sky.

When I'm as grown-up as Mommy,

I will be practical *and* creative.

I will know exactly
which notes to play.

And how to grow
my own food.

When I grow up,
I will have lots of adventures.

Mommy says there
are **fantastic** days...

...and **frustrating** days.

We get things wrong sometimes,

but we *always* find reasons to laugh!

Mommy says we all do things we regret.

Sometimes a **cuddle**
is all you need to feel better.

All my friends think Mommy is **awesome**, especially at parties.

She's great at hiding treasure,

sharing ice cream
(most of the time),

and all kinds of joining in!

When I grow up,
I'm going to be
just like Mommy.

Because no matter how clever she seems…

…Mommy is always ready for fun,

just like me!